Goldie Socks
and the
Three Libearians

Jackie Mims Hopkins

Illustrations by John Manders

Fort Atkinson, Wisconsin

For my Aunt Kathy, who still loves to read in book tents and for my friend, Julie Cowan, who knows how to find books that are "just right." Thank you to Melanie Scales and her son, Will, who were there when Goldie's spark began.
—J. M. H.

For Heather and Steven Jr.
—J. M.

Published by UpstartBooks
W5527 State Road 106
P.O. Box 800
Fort Atkinson, Wisconsin 53538-0800
1-800-448-4887

Text © 2007 by Jackie Mims Hopkins
Illustrations © 2007 by John Manders

Once upon a time ...

nestled deep in an enchanted forest, there lived a book lovin'
bear family. Papa bear was a public libearian, Mamma bear was
a school libearian, and their son, Baby bear, was a libearian in
training at the Grizz Lee Preschool.

One morning, a little girl named Goldie Socks was on her way to school. Goldie Socks usually walked along the road, but this day, since she was running particularly late, she decided to take a shortcut through the forest.

By and by, Goldie Socks came upon an astonishing
sight—there, in the middle of the forest, she saw a cottage
that appeared to be made of books!

Goldie Socks loved books more than bears love honey, so she went up to the house for a closer look. She knocked on the door, and, to her surprise, it creaked open.

Cautiously, Goldie Socks peeked inside. Shelves and shelves of wondrous books lined the walls. She called out to see if anyone was home, but no one answered. Goldie Socks knew she shouldn't go in, but the temptation of all those books was more than she could bear.

Once inside the cottage, Goldie Socks went straight to the shelves and began browsing through the books. The first book she pulled off the shelf was too big. In fact, it was so heavy it fell on the floor.

Goldie Socks went to another shelf, but the book she took from this shelf was too little. Then she looked through some nonfiction books and found one that was **just right**.

Goldie Socks wandered over to another shelf and opened up a chapter book. She used the five finger rule to see if the book was too hard. She started with a closed fist. When she came to a word she couldn't read, she put one finger up.

All five fingers went up while reading the first
page of the book, so she knew that book
was too hard for her. She tried another
book, but it was too easy. Then she
found a book of fairy tales that
was **just right**.

After she found several books that were **just right** for her, Goldie Socks began searching for the perfect place to read them.

Goldie Socks looked around the room and spotted a big Lazy Bear recliner. She climbed up in the enormous chair and pushed back, but it went back too far.

She surveyed the room again, and this time she spied a poofy couch with lots of pillows.

Goldie Socks sprang into the air and landed smack dab in the middle of the couch. Pillows flew everywhere! The couch was too squishy. Maybe there is a comfy place upstairs, she thought.

When Goldie Socks reached the top of the stairs, she saw a tent
made out of a blanket. She crawled inside the cozy tent,
opened the book of fairy tales, and began reading.

Yes, this place was **just right**.

Around noon, the three libearians came home for lunch.

Papa libearian immediately noticed one of his books on the floor. "Somebody's been looking at my big books and left one on the floor," he said. Then Mamma libearian said, "Somebody's been looking at my little books and put one back on the shelf with the pages showing instead of the spine." Then Baby libearian said, "Somebody's been looking at my nonfiction books, and one is gone!"

Papa libearian looked at another shelf and said, "Somebody's
been looking at my hard books and left one on top of the shelf."

"Somebody's been looking at my easy books and put one
back on the shelf upside down," said Mamma libearian.

Then Baby libearian said, "Somebody's been looking at
my fairy-tale books, and one is gone!"

Papa libearian saw that his favorite chair was not in the same position that he had left it. "Somebody's been sitting in my recliner and left it pushed back," he said.

Then Mamma libearian said, "Somebody's been on my poofy couch and knocked all the pillows on the floor."

The three libearians crept up the stairs. When they got to the top, Baby libearian said, "Somebody's been in my cozy reading tent, and there she is!"

Goldie Socks looked up from her book and saw the big sharp teeth of the three libearians …

... smiling at her.

Papa, Mamma, and Baby libearian joined Goldie Socks in
the tent. Papa libearian read a story to everyone ...

... and it was just right!